RACHEL
AN ELEPHANT
TREE CHRISTMAS
LYNNE KOSITSKY

**Look for the other Rachel stories
in Our Canadian Girl**

RACHEL
AN ELEPHANT
TREE CHRISTMAS
LYNNE KOSITSKY

PENGUIN
CANADA

PENGUIN CANADA

Published by the Penguin Group

Penguin Group (Canada), 10 Alcorn Avenue, Toronto, Ontario, Canada M4V 3B2
(a division of Pearson Penguin Canada Inc.)

Penguin Group (USA) Inc., 375 Hudson Street, New York, New York 10014, U.S.A.
Penguin Books Ltd, 80 Strand, London WC2R 0RL, England
Penguin Ireland, 25 St Stephen's Green, Dublin 2, Ireland (a division of Penguin Books Ltd)
Penguin Group (Australia), 250 Camberwell Road, Camberwell, Victoria 3124, Australia
(a division of Pearson Australia Group Pty Ltd)
Penguin Books India Pvt Ltd, 11 Community Centre, Panchsheel Park, New Delhi – 110 017, India
Penguin Group (NZ), Cnr Airborne and Rosedale Roads, Albany, Auckland, New Zealand
(a division of Pearson New Zealand Ltd)
Penguin Books (South Africa) (Pty) Ltd, 24 Sturdee Avenue, Rosebank, Johannesburg 2196,
South Africa

Penguin Books Ltd, Registered Offices: 80 Strand, London WC2R 0RL, England

First published 2004

1 2 3 4 5 6 7 8 9 10 (WEB)

Copyright © Lynne Kositsky, 2004
Cover and full-page interior illustrations © Ron Lightburn, 2004
Chapter-opener illustrations © Janet Wilson, 2004
Design: Matthews Communications Design Inc.
Map © Sharon Matthews

Manufactured in Canada.

LIBRARY AND ARCHIVES CANADA CATALOGUING IN PUBLICATION

Kositsky, Lynne, 1947–
Rachel : an elephant tree Christmas / Lynne Kositsky.

(Our Canadian girl)
"Rachael, book four".
ISBN 0-14-301671-7

I. Title. II. Title: Elephant tree Christmas. III. Series.

PS8571.O85R333 2004   jC813'.54   C2004-903060-4

Visit the Penguin Group (Canada) website at **www.penguin.ca**

For Leona,
dearest friend and agent, without whom
Rachel would never have existed

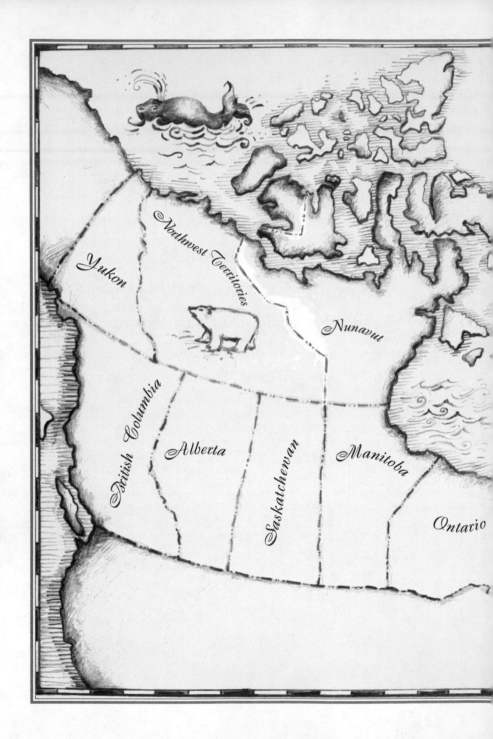

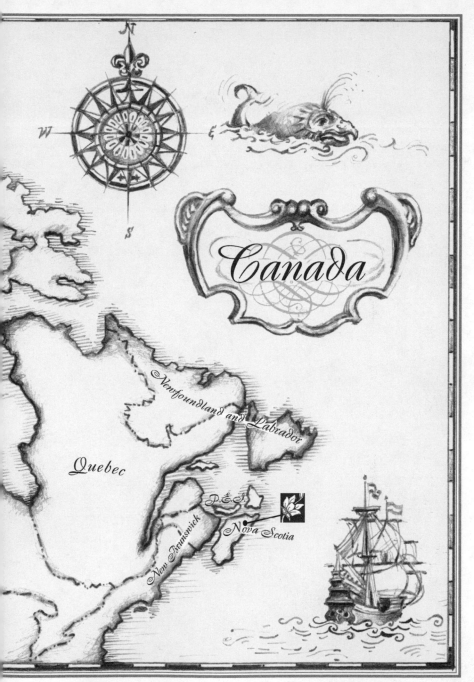

Canada

Newfoundland and Labrador

Quebec

P.E.I.

Nova Scotia

New Brunswick

 Marks the location of the story

RACHEL'S STORY CONCLUDES

W HEN THE REVOLUTIONARY WAR BEGAN in the American colonies, the British promised freedom to slaves who escaped to join them. By 1783 the war was over and the British had lost. They moved the ex-slaves, known as Black Loyalists, up to their remaining colonies. Many of these Loyalists were sent to Nova Scotia.

Rachel Sparrow moved to Birchtown, Nova Scotia, with her mother, Sukey. There they joined Rachel's stepfather, Titan. They spent their first winter in a cold and miserable pit-cabin, where Rachel's brother, Jem, was born. In the spring Titan built a wooden house for them in the small black area of Shelburne, a mostly white town, and the family moved. The house, their Maybe House, was a delight, but there was unrest in Shelburne. In the summer of 1784 during a terrible riot, white de-listed soldiers destroyed the new houses in the black neighbourhood and drove the inhabitants out of town.

Sorrowfully, the little family moved back to their crowded pit-cabin, while Titan began work on a new hut down by the shore. Colonel Blucke, the unofficial leader of Birchtown who lived in a big imposing house also near the shore, lent him building tools. The colonel had been in charge of a company of black pioneers when they'd first settled in Birchtown, and now he hired them out. Involved in most of the business of the town, he had the respect of everyone.

One day, while out in the woods gathering fruit, Rachel and Sukey were waylaid by a shabby soldier, Serjeant Gyssop, who kidnapped them and stole their precious certificates of freedom. He marched them through the woods and sold them back into slavery, Sukey to his brother, George, and Rachel to a new massa and missus, Mr. and Mrs. Pritchard. Mrs. Pritchard was very ill. At first she didn't trust Rachel, but later came to understand that the girl was a "free Negro." When Mrs. Pritchard realized that her illness had worsened and she was dying, she forced her husband to set Rachel free and to give her five golden guineas in wages. In the fall Rachel found her way back to Birchtown. But as book four begins, Rachel's mother, Sukey, is still missing.

CHAPTER N⁰ 1

"All this work," sniffed Rachel. *"You'd* never think there'd be so much of it in such a narrow little dark place. I spend all my time huffing and puffing." She dragged a kettle of water to the fire. It sloshed sideways, so she dispersed some of the spillage around the floor with her bare foot. Droplets raced across the wooden boards like ants, vanishing double-quick into corners. It was almost as good as sweeping, she persuaded herself, which she didn't have the time or inclination for right now.

Here they lived, Rachel and Titan and Jem in

their new hut, a small log cabin down by the shore of Birchtown. Titan hadn't given up after their disaster in Shelburne. He had fashioned every log and seam of this new home himself. It wasn't the Maybe House, it could never be that, but it was a kind of house all the same, with one small room and a fireplace to cook on and keep them passably warm—as long as there was enough wood chopped. Rachel felt she mustn't be ungrateful—it was much better than the pit-cabin, anything had to be better than that—but sometimes it was hard to keep the tears from squeezing out and running down her nose when her hands were rough and aching from the labour of it all.

Mamma was still lost, and Rachel felt lost without her. It wasn't just a question of love. And it wasn't just that Mamma was the twine that tied them neatly into a family bundle. It was more than that. Truth told, Rachel found it dreadfully hard being the mamma in Mamma's place, doing all the woman chores and looking after the baby besides. Though she'd never have admitted it before, it was even harder not to hear Mamma's grumping day after day. The lack of it meant her warm stout presence was gone and Rachel was supposed to act the grown-up woman of the house. Now it was just Titan and herself to guard Jem against the harsh befallings of the world.

She didn't feel ready for it. She wanted normal child chores and the freedom to be out in the woods with her Micmac friend, Ann-Marie, or even better, she wanted to be sitting on a rock, book-studying. Or putting memorized tricky things into little Corey's head, reading and arithmetic, to make Nanna Jacklin's grandson into a civilized Nigra. She needed to give those tricks away, pass them along like a great chain of learning. First to Corey, then to her own little brother, Jem, when he was big enough, and then, who knew? Learning, reading and writing, could just stretch and stretch like a great fishing net till it covered the world. And everyone fished up in that net would be happier for it, doubtless.

Thinking about Mamma again, Rachel went over it all in her mind, just as she'd done nearly every day since Mamma had been gone. She'd racked and riddled her brains and told Titan all she knew. Rachel was a good describer. But no one, not Titan, not Nathan Crowley, not even the Sunday preacher who came sometimes to Birchtown but travelled around the whole area, had been able to search Mamma or her captor, George Gyssop, out. Now the Micmac family of Ann-Marie were seeking. They used their wits and their eyes and small bunches of herbs and stones to divine by, but though it was said that they could find anyone or anything, that they could find a lone white crab in the whole wide ocean, they'd not found Mamma. Maybe Gyssop had moved on, taking her with him, his property.

Rachel tried to remember more. Her missus Pritchard in Shelburne had said George Gyssop was likely named after King George of England, but a man less like a king you'd be hard put to find.

"You've done your best. That's the truth," replied Titan, when she told him that last tidbit of knowledge, and there was the end to it. But he had a wild lost look, and every night he sat with his arms dangling and his chin dropped almost all the way to his chest.

The hut had chinks in the log walls, filled with straw, bits of paper, and scraps of fabric the family had found to keep the wind out. There wasn't much thrown away in Birchtown. Almost every last fragment of anything was used up. Yet there were still gaps in the walls for the gale, when it visited, to whistle through. This wasn't entirely bad. A space between two logs near the door made a bit of a hidey-hole for keeping things in. Rachel thought of it as her treasure trove. Not that she had a pile of things to store there. But she did have something special: the five English guineas. Rachel had pushed the precious coins under some straw in the hole, wanting to keep them for the worst days of winter. Then they'd shine like summer sun. Then they'd be more useful than a spade to dig taters, more useful even than the biggest basket in the world for *bluebetties,* and then some. She didn't tell anyone about them, not Ann-Marie, not Titan, not Nathan Crowley. They were her secret.

Rachel had never seen nor known such money in her life before. Each heavy drop of gold was worth twenty-one shillings, more than she could carry in her hand at one time or fold her mind around. She tried doing the sums, using the numbers that Nathan had taught her. One guinea was a nest egg; five a fortune, likely more than Titan could earn in half a year—and that was if there was work for him. There'd been little enough lately, skilled carpenter though he was.

Sometimes Rachel caught a glint of the hidden coins in the straw of the wall, especially after the wind blew hard, and covered them fast, her fingers trembling and dark against the spangly cool yellowness of them. They were a secret spell. They lifted the Sparrows from the level of the other Nigras roundabout and set them somewhere else. In their way they were now high and mighty maybe as Colonel Blucke, the head of Birchtown. Thinking that made her feel guilty and good at the same time—she was keeping something back from Titan, it was true, but in the end it would be something for all of them. Her coins were the guinea promise. They drifted luminous and spanking clean through her dreams. Somehow she imagined they would keep the family safe from the bad people that still hung around Birchtown, the de-listed soldiers and the homeless drifters. She didn't know where those folk came from. She didn't know what they kept locked up in their minds. It frightened her.

But, "Here we are, Titan," she was finally going to say one day around Christmas, her chest puffed like a pigeon, if things became too hard to bear. "Here's all we need to buy the fish and grain to get us through these mis'rable times."

And Titan would stare at her and grin, and they'd all dance round in a circle, singing and laughing. Negro frolicks, the white folk would call their antics, with that lordly toss of the head. But Rachel knew better. It was just pure energy that needed to be let out, like steam from the cooking pot, and a bit of the fear as well. Best of all, when Rachel came to think back on it, Mamma was in those imaginings too, singing and laughing with the rest of them.

The new Sparrow hut was a little ways along from the big rich house of Colonel Blucke, and Titan always tipped his cap to him of a morning, especially as Colonel Blucke had loaned him tools to make their new hut. Colonel Blucke wasn't white or black. He was somewhere in between, a nice tan colour like he was white folk sunned too long, and that made him special. He'd been mighty important during the war, an army officer in charge of many Nigras. A kind man, though gruff enough to put the shyness into Rachel whenever she passed him, he still organized the men into work brigades whenever possible and bargained with the white authorities back in Shelburne over food and pay. But all Colonel Blucke's effort didn't seem to help a titch at the moment. Rations were cut, the Nigras were facing more starvation than they'd ever borne as slaves, and you could actually hear winter most days, whining round corners and rattling ill-fitting doors. Or even worse, pit-cabin roofs. "I'm coming," it seemed to be moaning. "You think things are bad now, but I'm coming, so watch out."

Rachel prayed it wouldn't be like last winter. The snow had been piled so high it covered the whole town, and all she'd seen when she went out were rows of spiralling smoke, issuing out of the ice—like men were puffing on their tobaccy pipes underneath. That was because the drifts had grown so tall all the chimneys and roof holes were hidden. Folk both black and white crossed themselves or spat sideways when they spoke of it. They prayed such cruel weather would never come again. But if it did there were still those five guineas. There were always the guineas. Come snow or hail or freezing weather too bad to tramp out in, the Sparrows would make it through the ice days. But Rachel didn't want the coins used up faster than needed, for after that there'd be nothing. And the feeling of having nothing made a big hurting hole in her middle like the worst kind of bellyache. So she had to figure out, careful as a squirrel hoarding for its long sleep, when and how to act, what to use the sparkling money for.

CHAPTER N° 2

"My turn to tell a story," smiled Ann-Marie. It was one of those strange mild days in late fall that squeezed themselves, flat and miraculous, between one sharp edge of wintry weather and another. Rachel wasn't exactly sitting listening, she didn't have the leisure for that, but she was spreading damp cleaning rags and Jem's few washed bits of clothes on a sun-warmed rock while cocking an ear to what her best friend was saying. It was so good to be together again, so good to see Ann-Marie smile, even if Rachel did have to work all the while.

It's amazing, she thought, *how many things you can do at the same time if you only put your mind to it.* Flat lengths of bark full of drying *cranbetties* lay in the sun, and angular wooden logs, with pale glistening edges that leaked slightly, stood heaped against the hut. Rachel had laid out the berries and then split the wood this morning against the cold that would no doubt pay another visit soon. Next time it came calling it would likely stay till spring, spreading out its snowy petticoats and settling in like the lady of a great house. She winced at the thought. Ann-Marie had helped her pile up the firewood, meanwhile explaining how berries could be crushed and dried with slivers of meat, maybe using wood smoke for the drying process, to make winter food.

"I don't think there'll ever be much meat in this house," replied Rachel sorrowfully. She hadn't eaten a bite of beef since returning from the Pritchards'. Then she thought of the guineas, each about the size of a man's thumbnail. "Broad pieces," she'd heard them called, but they looked anything but broad to her. Perhaps she could buy a whole cow with the coins and then there'd be milk and meat. But she knew it wasn't the best way to spend them. Cows had to be fed, after all. And once you'd eaten the meat there'd be no more milk. That was the way of things, sure enough, as Titan would say.

"Story, story," cried Corey, who was hanging around as usual, doing nothing that could be called useful. "But no more spider stories, please." He was still an annoyance, but it was a gladness to Rachel that he said *please* and that he was beginning to speak properly. Perhaps something could be done with him after all.

"Kisiku'k wikuombk ..." began Ann-Marie.

"What's that mean?" Corey demanded. Two or three other Nigra children had crept close to hear. Jem, who had hauled himself upright, was hanging on to Ann-Marie's shoulder as she sat on the ground cross-legged. A bit wobbly on his feet, he was staring straight into her face, concentrating. He was also drooling, with all the new teeth coming through. Looking around her, Rachel suddenly had an idea: this would make a good learning group. Another time, when Ann-Marie wasn't storytelling, perhaps Rachel could teach the Nigra children that letters might have horns or curlicues or look like broken splinters of wood, but when it came right down to it, they all meant something important.

Colonel Blucke marched by, actually tipping *his* hat to *them,* rather than the other way round, as if they were grown-up important people. Not that most of them had hats, of course.

"Good mornin', Colonel Blucke," chorused the children, who had been taught on all accounts to be polite to him. But the colonel had already disappeared into his big house.

"Kisiku'k wikuombk ... it's how we begin a story. It tells how everyone is sitting listening. That might be a lesson for *you,"* Ann-Marie told Corey, who was flexing his toes, worrying an ant, and scratching his head. "It's not another spider story, don't worry, nor the story of Rabbit and

Moon, though that will be good for another time. It's a child story."

There was a rustle in the small stand of trees above the shore, perhaps folk coming through, but for the moment Rachel paid little heed, though she felt a quick squeeze of the heart. New Nigras were always crossing and recrossing Birchtown, tramping down to the shore or through the forests with a kind of longing in them. Times were bad, Nigras were unwanted over in Shelburne, and so men and women were forever looking for a staying place. If she got mixed up with them, with their hoping and wanting, she'd soon be thinking more about their troubles than those of her own family. So she was growing hard. Her eyes would glitter when she saw the ragtag strangers, perhaps from frozen tears, but she'd ignore both her tears and the people. They always had a certain set to their shoulders, like they were being pulled down into the earth, life being too heavy for them, but there was nothing she could do about it.

"There was, in the old times, an old woman and an old man," Ann-Marie began. "They were very poor. One day they heard a great banging from under the earth and went to see what it was. A tiny hand came up and they yanked on it, hard, hard, till a little boy burst up through the ground like a young shrub."

"Was he from a pit-cabin?" asked one of the Nigra girls, whose nickname was Molasses because her face was always sticky. She lived in a little pit-cabin herself, her family was that poor.

"Kind of. He was from the middle of the earth. A spirit place."

"I bet the old man and the old woman were mighty surprised," said Rachel.

Another rustle. She stared up at the trees for a moment but could see nothing. Maybe it wasn't Nigra folk after all, but a bear or a wolf in the pines. Or even worse, a de-listed soldier. The small circle of children harkening to the Indian story were safe enough here. They could run inside the Sparrow hut and bolt the door if threatened, though it would make for a massive crowd. There was always one kind of danger or another. *Calm yourself, girl,* she told herself in Mamma's voice. She was too fanciful for her own good.

"Mighty surprised," replied Ann-Marie, who had noticed nothing amiss, "but however poor you are, you can't just throw away children. So they took him home and looked after him. He grew very fast, as boys always do, and the old man and the old woman, who became poorer and poorer with each passing day, had a great deal of trouble feeding him."

The children nodded. This was something they understood.

There was definitely something in those trees, and Rachel felt that whatever it might be was aimed directly at her, or at them all, maybe. That was the way her imagination worked. A dark cloud darted across the sun like an arrow spun from a bow, and she clenched her fists. Ann-Marie looked up, mildly surprised.

"Something wrong?" she murmured.

"Not sure," Rachel whispered back. She turned to the children. There were at least fifteen of them now, too many to fit into the hut. They'd drifted by, two or three at a time, eager to hear the Micmac story. "I think we should save the rest of this tale for another day. Is it a good place to stop, Ann-Marie?"

"A very good place." Ann-Marie took her cue from Rachel. "Can you imagine what's going to happen next?" she asked the children. They shook their heads.

"Maybe I'll start to teach you Nigras your letters next time we meet," Rachel went on. "Till it gets too cold, this can be our schoolhouse, right by this big bush. Ann-Marie can tell tales, I can teach reading and writing, and Corey—" Rachel stared at the grubby child with disapproval "—will show us all how to wash our faces and comb our hair. We could meet every second day except church day."

"Aw, I wanna hear rest of story now." Corey rubbed his nose. "I don' wanna wait."

"Time is jus' an arm long. You can reach clean across it." Rachel was borrowing one of Mamma's mysterious sayings. There was never any arguing with what Mamma said. Most folk didn't understand her anyhow, though she sounded fancy. Rachel thought the saying might just shut Corey up, and it did, though he commenced to scratch his head again. "You all go home now," continued Rachel. She said goodbye to Ann-Marie, picked up Jem, and hurried into the house, shutting the door. She really didn't want to know who or what was in those trees.

CHAPTER N.º 3

It didn't take her long to find out. Five minutes or so later there came a hard impatient knocking at the door.

"It's a person, then, that's for sure. Bears and wolves don't knock." But she made no move to open it.

Titan was out on a rare day of carpentering, and she was all alone with Jem. It could be a white soldier, looking to make some mischief. She shuddered. She'd had her fill of *them*.

The banging grew more insistent. "Who's there?" she cried, her voice wavy as a swath of seaweed.

"It's me, Rachel, Nathan Crowley. Could you please open the door? Way things are, with Nigras hating whites and vice versa, this bain't the best place to be."

Greatly relieved, Rachel drew up the latch. "You should say, 'It is I,' not, 'It's me,'" she corrected, unable to resist, as soon as she saw him. Theirs was a who-could-best-whom kind of friendship. "That's what you taught me."

"Oh, for heaven's sake. This is important. You want to hear, or d'you prefer to go on correcting my grammar?" He ducked into the house.

"Mamma?" she breathed. "Is it Mamma? Have you found her?"

"No, this is not about your mother. It's about ... Hannah."

"Hannah?" Hannah was the Crowleys' slave. What had she to do with Rachel?

There was a slight rustle, like the noise in the trees earlier. Nathan glanced sideways and back, gave a short whistle, and Hannah crept over from her hiding place. "We there, Miz Rachel, in them trees, watchin' you with they children." A sorry sight, Hannah, tired-eyed and bedraggled, slouched behind Nathan, her face peeping round his left shoulder.

What were they doing here together? What on earth was the matter? Rachel couldn't believe Missus Crowley would allow her slave to go gallivanting through the wild lands between Shelburne and Birchtown. She had duties at home. Then she realized: Hannah was carrying a small damp bundle wrapped in a rag, as though she were free to be journeying.

"She fell in a stream," Nathan offered helpfully, as if this explained everything. "I fished her out."

"'Tweren't my fault, Massa Nathan. It black as hell in that there forest."

Rachel looked from one to the other of them with amazement, and Jem climbed up and hugged Nathan's knees.

"What are you both doing here?" Rachel asked finally, fit to burst with curiosity. "Did something dreadful happen? Did your house burn down?"

"My parents turned Hannah out."

"What?"

"Times are bad, our rations have been cut, and many owners are getting rid of their slaves before winter comes. They're all over the streets of Shelburne. My parents say they won't be able to feed Hannah and us as well, so they're letting her go."

"I free, Miz Rachel." Hannah sounded doleful as a dog on a wet and windy day.

Rachel, in return, was speechless as a duck with all its quacks used up. This didn't seem like a good kind of free.

After staring at his silver-buckled shoes for a moment and taking care to meet nobody's gaze, Nathan took Rachel aside and whispered to her, "I know things are hard, but could she stay here?"

"How're we expected to afford her keep if your rich family can't?" she whispered back. "Our rations, what there were of them, have been cut too." She would have hated for Hannah to hear her, but it had to be said.

"I don't know. But with no family, with no logic or wit about her, the girl won't survive on her own for long."

That was true enough. Although it bruised Rachel's brain to think badly of her, Hannah didn't have the sense of a flea, had actually liked being a slave.

"D'you have any money?" Rachel asked Hannah. "Did they pay you off?" She almost added, "Like Massa Pritchard paid me," but stopped herself just in time. Best not to go sliding over that cliff.

"No'um. They say, 'You free now. Hannah. Look what we done for you. Take you baggage and go.' But I don' have no baggage."

"Nothing at all?"

"Only what I standin' up in, Miz Rachel, and this here little bundle, wi' a crust of bread in it. I bet it all wet now." Hannah wasn't standing up in much, a chemise and dust-stained skirt, no shoes. Nathan had the grace to look ashamed.

"Do *you* have any money?" Rachel asked him.

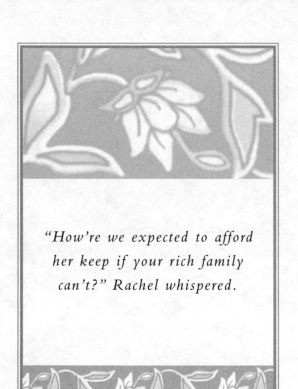

"How're we expected to afford her keep if your rich family can't?" Rachel whispered.

"No. Only my pocket money, and I spent that on maple-sugar apples before I knew this was going to happen."

"Maple-sugar apples. Huh. Some people don't know they're born, sure enough." Rachel felt higher and mightier than Nathan Crowley for a moment. Times might be hard, but he still spent his coins on candy. Then she looked at both him and Hannah in despair. This problem would take a mountain of chewing over. She thought and she thought, her mind arguing with itself like white folks and Nigras having a quarrel. Suddenly she had a glimmer of an idea. "Go into that corner, both of you, and warm your hands by the fire."

"I'm not cold," Nathan said testily.

"Never mind. Take yourself over there and do as you're told." In the past Rachel could never have imagined speaking like this to Nathan. But somehow now, as an extension of his mean family, he didn't deserve better. And she wasn't done yet. "Whatever you do, don't turn your head around, for I've a lifesaver of a plan. You neither, Hannah. Keep your eyes glued on those embers."

"Yessum." Hannah scuttled across to the fireplace, Jem crawling after her. To Rachel's relief, Nathan followed, his head down. Sometimes whites couldn't think up any better schemes than Nigras, it appeared, though they had a heap more schooling.

As soon as she was sure neither of them was watching, Rachel darted over to her hidey-hole. She shifted a bit of straw, her heart hammering. But there they still were, precious and untouched, her very own guineas, small and round and golden. They glittered in the narrow bar of sun that shone in a white blaze through the door. Almost unwillingly, loath to touch it, knowing it would be a parting touch, she took one of them out. It glittered in her palm and she grasped it tightly. Four. Now there would be four. She covered the others. There was still a great store of money to get the Sparrow family through the winter.

"Nathan, look here." She unclasped her hand.

He stared at the small coin in wonder. "A broad piece. A King George guinea. More than I ever had. Where in heaven or earth did you get that?"

"Never you mind. It's my money. I got it fair and square." She'd learned that phrase from Serjeant Gyssop. His shadow passed over her and she shivered as she said it. There was a moment's hush as they all stared at the guinea, Hannah's eyes near popping out of her head. Then Rachel spoke again. "I want you to take this coin, Nathan, and use it for us. Every so often you're to go to the store of that nasty white woman— the one who looks like she has a bad smell under her nose—in Shelburne, and bring food here for the winter."

"Why don't you do it? You're the one with all the money." Nathan sounded snotty.

"I can't. She won't serve me if I don't have a white massa. Don't fetch nothing fancy, just potatoes and meal and other fill-the-belly kinds of food. That way I can tell Titan that Hannah is living here but you're looking out for her. That way he'll be thinking she's not costing us a penny nor a three-penny piece. It's our only hope."

Nathan promised. And that only left Titan to go along with having Hannah live with them. They argued that night. Titan couldn't understand why the Crowleys would have a slave but keep her somewhere else.

"I not a slave no more. I free," Hannah moaned.

Titan looked at her sharply, but Rachel had practised her answer over and over again. "The Crowleys had no room for her. It's just that Nathan Crowley feels guilty, and he knows we're poor, so he's helping out."

"Harrumph." Titan was beginning to sound like Mamma. But as he muttered nothing else, just sat in his rickety chair, pushing it onto its two back legs with his eyes shut, Rachel took it they had a deal.

Hannah was a rare nuisance to have around. She was like a shadow Rachel couldn't shake. But the girl did carry Jem around on her hip, and she did bank the fire, and she did help with all the other chores, and that, Rachel felt, was maybe worth a hundred guineas in the scheme of things. But she had to get Hannah to stop saying "Miz Rachel" and "Yessum" all the time. It made Rachel feel like a slave owner.

CHAPTER N.º 4

"What a crowd!" Rachel exclaimed with a mix of gladness and dread as she went outside. She more or less had to drag Hannah with her. Hannah didn't believe in "the book-learnin'" for slaves or ex-slaves or Nigras in general. She thought "them things" too uppity. But she'd come anyway, to hang on to Jem and make sure he didn't get in the way. Maybe, with a little luck and a lot of trying, some tiddly-bit of knowledge would squirm its way into her brain.

The day was real nippy, but a bunch of children were there anyhow, waiting by the big bush outside the Sparrow hut. Rachel had given maybe five lessons so far, and word had spread like beef fat on bread. There must have been about thirty children now, all eager for stories and lessons. It was pretty amazing, but a mite daunting too, all those pairs of eyes fixed on hers and expecting so much from her. Rachel wondered if she had enough learning stored in her brain for them, but she was bent on teaching them whatever she knew. Still, there wouldn't be too many more days of class, for there was already frost on the ground and the snow would come soon. It hung like a great grey-white sheet over Birchtown, ready to drop down and cover the land. Many of the Nigra children had no coats or shoes. As it was they sat huddled against each other for warmth, their small faces bleak. The makeshift school would have to stop for the winter and that would be a great pity. Because learning was freedom. Rachel had drummed it into them till their ears burned, and not with cold neither.

Ann-Marie had come today and was just about to finish her story. She was hurrying it along so that Rachel would have time to teach another batch of her curlicue letters or numbers before the snow enveloped the little gathering. It was already beginning to spill out of the sky, plump flakes light and white as goose feathers.

"So," said Ann-Marie after reminding them of the beginning of the Micmac tale, "the boy knew that the old couple couldn't afford to feed him. They had barely enough for themselves. In fact the whole Micmac village was poor and the people hungry as slaves, so the boy decided to become a hunter. He hunted on land, he hunted at sea, but no one had taught him, and he didn't have much luck."

"He needed to be learnt things, like we are," interrupted Corey. Rachel beamed at him with surprise and pride.

"Just so," Ann-Marie went on. "But with the help of the old man, he made himself a bow and arrow and a harpoon. He practised and practised and practised on old stumps of trees and bushes and such. One day, thinking that perhaps he'd practised enough, he saw a great whale in the sea and caught it all by himself. He dragged it onto the beach and ran to fetch the old couple. Then the old lady took a knife and cut the whale up, making sure to throw its bones back into the ocean so it would grow again. Now there was plenty of food for the boy, the old couple, and the whole village, right through the winter."

"Wish we could catch a whale," Molasses said sadly. She looked hungry and pinched, and her face was quite dry and smooth, like there wasn't any more treacle in her house.

They all sighed. Quickly Rachel picked up a stick and began to draw letters in the soil and first flakes of snow. D E F. "They're the second lot of letters in the alphabet. This is the noise they make." She sounded them out. "What did I teach you last time?"

"A B C," called out a little boy in the back.

"Well done," came a deep growly voice. Rachel jumped. It was Colonel Blucke, fresh out of his fancy house down the shore. He was wearing his long coat, a cocked hat, and carrying a cane.

"Rachel? You Titan's girl?"

"Yessuh." She sounded like Hannah, but Colonel Blucke was a big important person in Birchtown. Even if you didn't know that, even if no one had ever told you, you'd work it out just by looking at him. Rachel could glimpse his shiny breeches buckles glinting out from under his coat, and the trace of a clean shirt ruffle around his neck. Colonel Blucke was rich as most white folk. You *could* say he was the mayor of Birchtown. And you wouldn't be far wrong.

"You're doing a fine job with these Negro children. Come and speak to me tomorrow afternoon."

"Yessuh, I will."

"When the sun reaches just past its highest point."

Rachel nodded.

And just like that, Colonel Blucke was gone along the path towards Shelburne, leaving Rachel quaking in the shoes that Missus Pritchard had given her. What on earth could someone as big and important as Colonel Blucke want with a little nobody of a Nigra like her?

There was a scratching at the door. Titan was out cutting wood, and Hannah had taken Jem down to where the sea met the pond to fill a pail with the blood-coloured water. Rachel was all by herself.

"Miz Rachel? You there? It's me, Molasses."

Rachel ran to let her in.

"I had to come. It was the story that Micmac girl told. We ain't got no food, Miz Rachel, not one scrap. Our supplies all run out, and those of the next-door folk too. There's six of us children all in that little pit hole with nothin' to eat. We gonna starve this winter, sure an' certain."

Rachel thought of the whale. She thought of how it fed the whole Micmac village and how its bones got thrown back into the sea to make more whale. She thought of the four golden guineas in her chink in the wall. Titan was bringing in a little money still. He was a skilled carpenter. They would manage somehow.

"Turn your back," she told Molasses sharply. Two minutes later, after a mighty shiver of worry and hesitation, Rachel gave Molasses a broad piece, shutting it tight into the other girl's hand before she changed her mind.

"What's this?" The girl, alarmed, peeked through the gaps in her fingers at the glint of gold that lay in her palm. She'd never seen anything half so brilliant or shiny before.

"It'll get you through the winter. Give it to your daddy. He'll know what to do with it."

"Yessum."

"And don't you go letting anybody know about it outside your family."

"No'um."

After Molasses left, grinning and crying, Rachel returned to her hidey-hole and counted the guineas. Now there were three. She had just wanted to make sure.

"Well," said the colonel as he folded one leg over the other and leaned back in his seat. "You surely are doing a good job with those Negro children hereabouts. I've been thinking of starting a school myself. Who taught you how to read?"

Rachel was drinking tea out of a pretty blue-and-white cup in Colonel Blucke's big house, trying not to choke. He had real furniture, and rugs, and shutters on the windows. Pretty glasses and patterned dishes were lined up on the shelves. The tea had streamed out of a big china teapot, and there were even slop and sugar bowls

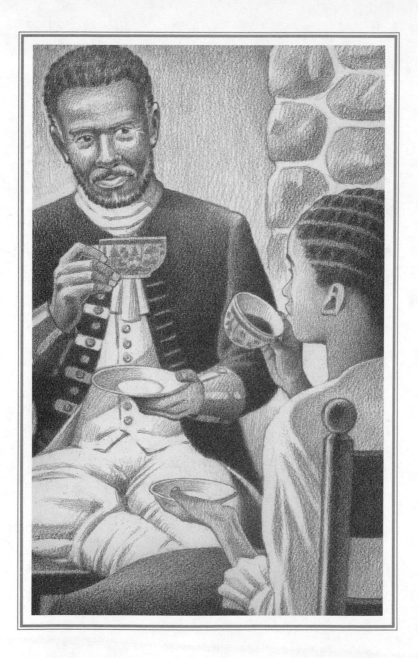

Rachel was drinking tea out of a pretty blue-and-white cup in Colonel Blucke's big house.

on the tray that sat on the table. It was difficult not to get distracted by the richness of the place.

She sat ramrod straight in her chair and concentrated real hard. "Nathan Crowley, a white boy, suh, and Missus Pritchard." She figured this needed some explaining, and she was worried as well about telling him that a white boy had taught her the alphabet. So she added a little more, first a sentence, then a sip of tea, then another sentence, then another sip, until the whole story was out in the open and the tea was nothing but dregs. She wouldn't have left that tea undrunk for anything. It had real cubes of sugar in it. And Mamma had once said that a tea leaf was just like a little shimmer of gold dust, worth about as much, too.

"A white boy?" asked the colonel, his eyebrows knitting together.

"Yessuh. I met him in the woods once, and he's been awful kind."

"Well, good for him and good for you. Teaching and learning, you could say, are as valuable as a drawer full of guineas."

Rachel swallowed hard, though there wasn't a jot of tea left, neither in her mouth nor in the cup.

"Anyway," said the colonel, changing the subject, "you can't go on teaching those little ones out there much longer. It's growing far too cold."

"Yessuh, you're right. I've been a heap worried over that. If we leave their learning till spring, they'll have forgotten mostly everything they know. Besides, it's hard enough to get the knowledge into their heads in the first place without most of it falling out again." Rachel was concerned that maybe she'd said too much, but felt she had to go on. "I'd teach them over the winter, but our house is much too small for all of them."

Colonel Blucke grinned a big wide friendly grin, and his eyes crinkled. "I've got a fine big house, with only me, my wife, and our servant knocking around in it. There's a large front entrance with no furniture of any value in it. You'll have seen it on your way in. You could teach those Negroes there."

"I could?"

"Yes, missy, and then maybe come the spring we'll build a real schoolhouse, like the white folk have over in Shelburne. I'll even throw in a bit of the teaching of the arithmetic myself. The Negro children need learning, same as everyone else."

"Now isn't that what I'm always saying? I'm sure they're just as clever deep down. You can't tell the depth of a well by the length of the pump-handle." A sudden tear dropped into her cup. She had sounded just like Mamma.

"Why, what is it, child?"

Rachel wavered for a moment. She really didn't know how much Colonel Blucke would want to hear, big important person that he was. But then she decided to go right ahead anyhow—what was the harm?—and tell him about picking *bluebetties,* and Serjeant and George Gyssop, and how Mamma had been taken back a slave. She had vanished just as surely as snow melted into spring streams.

"I know about that already. Just about every-one all the way to Shelburne knows it." The colonel looked grim, his wide smile suddenly shrunk to a narrow slash across his face, and for a moment Rachel felt she'd done wrong to bring the matter up in the first place. But the colonel soon turned back to the business of learning.

"You'll need to go from hut to hut and from one pit-cabin to the next to let the children know they'll be taught here. You teach *them,* and when I've time for it, I'll teach *you,* further your education a little. Now, how would that be?"

"That would be very fine, suh. And my Micmac friend, Ann-Marie?"

"She's welcome too. I think she's entitled to a bit of learning." He had said nothing about Mamma, so Rachel reckoned she shouldn't say anything more either. Instead she murmured her goodbyes and stammered out her thanks. Two minutes later she was on her way to fetch Hannah, who was cleaning out the grate in the fireplace. She quickly told her what was what. Then the two of them, swinging Jem between them, rushed from house to house and one pit-cabin to another in the early snow, telling all the Nigra children that there'd be school the next morning and every day till Christmas, excepting church days. And there was much clapping of hands and dancing up and down, and many a broad grin on a thin face. Though Hannah was quick to say afterwards that all this learning taxed a Nigra's brains something awful and she couldn't see, all things taken into account, why it was held to be such a good idea.

CHAPTER N.º 6

It had been a horrible morning. All Rachel had ever really wanted was to learn to read and write, and work out how to teach other Nigras, so they'd all have a chance, but now she saw that the second part of her dream, teaching the Nigra children, was going to be much harder than she'd reckoned on. She hadn't the training for it, perhaps not the talent either. About thirty-five had turned up, eager to learn, or see what was what, or just cause trouble—maybe because it was too cold to play outside. Worst of all, Ann-Marie was nowhere to be found, perhaps too shy to come into the fancy place.

At first mostly all the children except a few bold boys were awed by the Blucke house and couldn't even stammer out so much as a word, not even an A or a B or a C, though somehow Corey had miraculously changed from the worst little nuisance into her star pupil. But quicker than it took to drink a cup of water, nearly all the children got rowdy as de-listed soldiers. Two boys pulled Molasses' hair till she cried, one boy punched another because his legs were in the way, two small girls pushed a third away from them, saying she smelled like a skunk, and Jem escaped Hannah, crawling into another room and smashing an expensive dish that belonged to the Bluckes. The noise quieted them all, but only for a second.

"See, I told you so," Hannah's eyes seemed to say, as if it wasn't her fault but Rachel's. Rachel thought maybe Hannah had let go of the baby on purpose because she didn't want to put up with all this "learnin' nonsense," as she put it, and besides, she looked about as innocent as a cat who'd just swallowed a mouse, tail and all. Rachel wanted to shake her hard, knock some sense or alphabet into her. Only Corey, quite amazingly, had been good, sitting on the floor with his face scrubbed and his hair slicked down like a proper little gentleman, patiently waiting to talk about the joys of being clean as havoc roared around him. Today he really *was* her star pupil.

Colonel Blucke poked his head around the door twice, both times when the racket was so bad it came back and punched Rachel in the face. She wanted to do something silly and violent, slap one of the children maybe, like the old slave missus on the plantation had slapped her. Instead, when she saw the colonel's face the second time, she bent down and pulled on her bootlaces so tight they snapped. It stopped her from doing something dreadful. Still, he would turn them out for sure now that he saw how wicked and unheeding the children were, how impossible it was for her to control them. But,

"You need to keep those Negroes busy," was all he said, mildly. "Don't let them rule the roost. I'll see if I can find some primers or hornbooks for them in Shelburne. It's the weather too. Bad weather makes for bad children."

As soon as class was over, Rachel parted company with Hannah and Jem and made for the woods. Frost slicked the path. It was freezing as February, and snow was blowing in vast fluffy clouds off the sea. But she had to be on her own for at least the length of a mockingbird's song. She just had to, or she'd never sort out her mind. Not that there were any mockingbirds around here. Why were the children so bad? Why couldn't they be more grateful? And who was she to think she could ever, ever teach them anything? "All this time you been thinking you Miss High and Mighty," she grumbled to herself, almost in Hannah's voice, "but truth to tell, you just the same as any other poor Nigra."

She was so busy scolding herself she barely noticed another girl standing in front of her.

"As if I haven't seen enough Nigra children for one day," she groaned. But then she stared in dismay. The child, although smaller and clearly younger than she was, seemed almost her mirror image, straight and tall with dark skin and tightly braided hair. Rachel could have sworn she was looking at herself, or at least, herself as she'd been three or four years back. She knew she should say something, but didn't know what.

"Hello," said the little girl. "I seed you coming out that big house. I been watching you."

She was dreadfully, painfully thin, Rachel realized, now that she was looking at the girl properly. One good gust would likely blow her away. "I haven't seen you before. What's your name?"

"Rachel," the girl replied promptly, and the bigger Rachel almost fainted.

"Why, that's my name too. I never did hear of any other Nigra having that name before. Where's your mamma and your daddy?"

"Further along in the woods." The girl jerked her head sideways as if to indicate where they might be found. "We just come to Birchtown. We was slaves before, but the massa threw us out."

"You from Shelburne?"

"No. Way, way east, my daddy says. We been walking long days."

And now that Rachel had gotten over her shock and come to think on it, the child did look tired as a dog that wouldn't leave off chasing its tail. But it was really none of Rachel's business. She couldn't be dealing with now-and-then folk, the passersby who came and went in Birchtown between one sneeze and another. She had enough problems of her own. She spun around and began running down the hill towards home.

"My mamma's awful sick," the girl cried after her. She didn't add, "Can you help any?" but Rachel knew only too well what she meant. And if there was one thing guaranteed to bring Rachel back, it was someone else's mamma being sick. Her own mamma had been sick too when they first came to Birchtown, sick almost to death, and Rachel had gone mad with worry. It had taken Ann-Marie's aunt with her Micmac ways and medicine bag to heal her. Rachel owed for that, she owed big. And sometimes you paid those kinds of debts by helping out someone else in the same kind of trouble. She sighed and turned slowly to face the girl.

"What's wrong with her?"

"Too much walking, no food. She's just bone-tired, can't get up."

"You'd better take me to see her," Rachel said. Her sigh was almost big enough to blow all the snow clouds out of the sky.

Little Rachel's mamma was lying flat out on a rock, her breath going into her with a sharp huff and coming back out again with a sharp puff. "Need some food," she whispered. Her eyes were

Little Rachel's mamma was lying flat out on a rock, her breath going into her with a sharp huff and coming back out again with a sharp puff.

closed and her eyelids had a bluish tinge to them. But it was at the little girl's daddy that Rachel stared most. He seemed tall as a mountain, even taller than Titan. He was dark and his limbs were straight and he looked familiar. It was as if Rachel had seen him before, perhaps in a dream.

"What be your name?" the man asked suddenly, drawing himself up higher than a pine tree. Rachel jumped.

"Rachel, suh," she said. He was the kind of person you just couldn't help saying "suh" to.

"And where you be from?"

"Down the hill in Birchtown, suh."

"No, I mean where you be from *before*."

"From New York, and before that, Charlestown, in South Carolina."

"What be your mamma's name?"

"Sukey, suh. Sukey Sparrow."

"I don't know about no Sparrow," said the man, "but I did know a Sukey once, long time ago, down in the South where they bring in the rice. I know'd her real well. She spoke those

African sayings real grand. And she had a little baby named Rachel, just like I call my young daughter here." The man's dark brown eyes went all blurry like he was crying.

And suddenly Rachel Sparrow understood. She didn't even have to figure it out. She had come face to face with her daddy. Her *real* daddy, not a stepdaddy like Titan. The daddy who'd been sold away from the plantation when she was very tiny. The daddy who was the reason she was so dark and straight and tall. He must have called his second daughter Rachel as a remembrance of her. By accident he'd found his way back to his first daughter. And Rachel could tell he knew that as well as she did.

"You come on down the hill with me," she said. "I'll give you what you need to buy as much food as you can eat. To make your wife a heap better and fatten up your daughter. And maybe you could even build a hut right here in Birchtown." She was thinking very hard. "You could stay near us in the meantime. There's a pit-cabin we used to live in that will do for a time. Mamma lives with Titan, my stepdaddy. She's gone for a while. But she'll be so pleased to see you when she gets back."

Rachel stopped, out of breath. She couldn't waste her brain space trying to figure out how to tell Titan that her real daddy was here. Or wondering what might happen when Mamma came back. *If* Mamma came back. Those were puzzles for the future. But she knew what she had to do right now. Little Rachel's mamma was starving, so there wasn't too much time. She would give two of the three remaining guineas to the little family, her mirror family. There were three of them after all, their plight was worse than anyone else's, and when everything was said and done the big tall man was her very own daddy. Afterwards she would have one guinea left. She didn't need Colonel Blucke to teach her more of the arithmetic to know that. Only one shining golden guinea would remain all by itself in her treasure trove, her little hidey-hole back at

the house. But it would be all right. It would have
to be. She, Titan, Jem, and even Hannah would
manage to get through the winter because every
now and then Nathan Crowley, true to his word,
was bringing them all kinds of cheap fill-the-belly
food from that bad-smell-under-the-nose storekeeper in Shelburne. They would all get by
somehow, new family and old. But she sighed.
She was ready to laugh and cry at the same time.
Her daddy, her real true daddy, was here. She'd
never thought to see him again. But thanks to
bumping into little Rachel on the hill, now she
had a new father and a new sister and a kind-of-
starving stepmother. In fact, she had an enormous
heap of people to worry her mind about.

Her family was growing and growing, spreading out branches, which put down roots, which
grew into new trunks. She was recollecting one
of those enormous banyan trees in Africa that
Mamma had once told her about. Banyan trees,
grey and many-footed, Mamma had said, were
the trapped spirits of elephants. If you waited

long enough, most likely when the moon was round and bright as one of Rachel's golden guineas and the night was young as Jem, you might surely see one of those trees pick up its roots and boughs and go tromping through the jungle.

An elephant tree, decided Rachel, who had seen neither a banyan nor an elephant in her entire life. Her family was an elephant tree. But she now had two daddies and had to figure out where each of them belonged in her scheme of things.

"Yes," said her new true daddy, interrupting her thoughts. "I come down the hill with you."

CHAPTER N.º 7

It was near Christmas. Ann-Marie had at last crept into classes at the big Blucke house.

"I didn't tell the whole story to the children," she whispered to Rachel. "Do you think I should?"

"What's left to tell?"

"That the old woman died, leaving the old man and the boy together."

"I think we might leave that part out," said Rachel. "There's been too much want and death for most of these Nigras already. Perhaps you could start on another story after I've taught them their M N O." But as she taught the unruly class their letters she came round to thinking scary thoughts about the story. The boy had caught the whale just as she had "caught" the golden guineas from the Pritchards. Then, in the Micmac tale, pieces of the whale had been given out to stop the village starving. She was doing the same kind of thing. She had given a guinea to Nathan Crowley to use for her family because Hannah was an extra mouth to feed. She had given a guinea to Molasses, whose face was all sticky again because there was treacle in her pit-cabin once more. And she had given two guineas to her new father so that his wife would recover and little Rachel would grow fat. She had sworn everyone to secrecy of course.

The old woman, a kind of mother to the boy in the story, had died when all the pieces of cut-up whale had been given out. Did that mean that Mamma was dead too, or at least that she would sure as sugar die if Rachel was stupid enough to give the last glittering guinea away? She shuddered, decided to keep that last guinea till the end of creation, no matter how hard up some folk in Birchtown might be, no matter how sad their tales of woe. It might be an imagining or it might really be a heap of bad luck to bestow it. She would keep it safe in the hidey-hole back at her house.

Colonel Blucke poked his head around the door, looking mighty serious. "I'm going away for a few days. I'm just about to saddle my horse and be gone. But you can keep on teaching right till Christmas Eve. My wife is here if you need anything." Then he poked his head back like a turtle going into its shell.

That meant no more of the arithmetic lessons for a while, but Rachel didn't really mind that. Although Colonel Blucke was a kind man, she didn't really like arithmetic, couldn't get the hang of subtracting or adding numbers above ten. She sure could count those guineas, though, that she had given away. She went through them yet again in her head.

She ended class early. As the Nigra children dispersed noisily, she began to walk along the shore to her home. A pile of untidy problems were growing into a mountain of trouble in her head. The students still made a racket louder than heaven's trumpet most of the time and would behave even worse with the colonel gone. One good glare of his usually simmered them down, but Rachel didn't have that kind of glare. On top of that she still hadn't told Titan about her new daddy and his family, who now lived in the Sparrows' old pit-cabin. And she still fretted like crazy about Mamma. She was worrying so hard she didn't even notice when little Corey, clean and neat, started to walk beside her.

"Miz Rachel?"

"Yes, Corey?"

"I sad."

"Why is that, Corey?"

"Can't tell you, Miz Rachel, not no-how. Nanna Jacklin told me not to tell no one."

"Oh dear," Rachel said. "I think you'd better tell me, Corey. You can't just say you're sad and then refuse to tell me why." From the look on Corey's gleaming scrubbed face she had a feeling she was about to hear very bad news indeed.

Corey hesitated.

"Go on, Corey. I really need to know."

"Nanna Jacklin will skin me if I tell."

"I'll skin you if you don't."

Corey gave a big sigh. "Well, Miz Rachel, there are no bebbies bein' born—at least not to rich ol' fambilies—and so Nanna Jacklin ain't bein' paid nothin'."

"Oh dear," Rachel said again.

"So we is hungry as a bear after winter, Miz Rachel. Only the water in the streams is free, and that's why I always looks so nice and clean, jus' like you told me to be."

Oh dear, oh dear, oh dear, Rachel thought, kicking a stone out of her way. *Mamma,* her heart screamed. *Corey and Nanna Jacklin,* her brain shouted. Somewhere along the line, without her even noticing, Corey and Nanna had become part of her family, the ears, perhaps, of her elephant tree. It was as if Mamma was on one side of an argument and Nanna Jacklin and Corey were on the other, as if they were being weighed against each other on the scales that the stuck-up storekeeper kept in her shop. For a moment Rachel couldn't make up her mind. What should she do? Mamma, if she was alive, was far away. There was no way Rachel could help her. Nanna Jacklin and Corey, on the other hand, were here, and they were starving. She could certainly change that. The scales tipped in their favour with a sad clang.

"You'd better come along with me," she said to Corey at last. "I have something that will help, but you're not to tell a soul in the whole wide world. Nanna Jacklin won't be cross with you, I promise, but she's not to tell a soul neither."

"Never, Miz Rachel. I'll makes sure she knows."

"Make," Rachel corrected him. "You'll *make* sure ..."

"Yessum," he replied solemnly. "I'll *make* sure she *know*."

Now not one guinea would remain. And it wasn't like throwing whale bones back in the water. No new guineas would grow. Suppose, in a mysterious kind of way, it affected Mamma? Suppose Mamma died? Rachel's heart dropped down to her toes. But more was to follow. The very next day.

CHAPTER N⁰ 8

"New folk living in our old pit-cabin," said Titan, breaking his usual silence.

"Yes, Titan." Rachel's pulse was fluttering in her throat, but she tried to sound like nothing was wrong. "They've been there awhile." Oh, why hadn't she told Titan the truth when she had the chance? She bit her lip.

Her stepdaddy was already out of his seat by the fireplace, slipping his long thin feet into his long thin shoes, and it didn't take too much imagining to guess he was on his way down there. Was he going to chuck them out into the snow? She couldn't bear to think of it.

"It's really cold," she ventured timidly, but he had that hard set look on his face that she had seen before. There was nothing for it but to go with him. Rachel tied her bootlaces, flung on her coat, and followed him. The snow was really deep now, creeping cold and wet inside the top of her boots.

With Titan's long stride and Rachel half running to keep up with him, it took much less time than she would have liked to reach the old cabin.

"Titan?"

"Um?"

And then Rachel told him. She told him her real true daddy lived in there. She told him about how sick his wife had been. She told him about her new sister. And then, just for good measure, as Mamma would say, she threw in the truth about the five golden guineas and how she'd given them all away, just like the boy in Ann-Marie's Micmac story had shared his pieces of whale with the whole village. Everything came out in a sorry rush.

"Five guineas?" Titan repeated, his eyes like stones. He must be working up to be very, very mad at her.

"Yes, Titan. I'm mighty sorry."

"Those people must have needed it more than we," was all he said. And he kept walking.

Now the trap door in the pit-cabin roof was just visible, and he knocked on it. Rachel remembered those miserable days in that old pit-cabin. She hoped the rest of her elephant tree family weren't doing too badly.

In a trice the trap door opened, and the head and shoulders of Rachel's daddy appeared. He was so tall that even with his feet planted on the pit-cabin floor, he still stood eye to eye with his daughter.

"Hello," he said, looking upwards from Rachel to Titan.

"Hello," replied Titan. "This was our cabin."

"Yes, I know."

Silence. Rachel was scared.

"Pretty uncomfortable. In spring, when the land comes unfrozen, I'll help you build a hut," Titan said fast and clipped, like he'd just made up his mind.

"Thank you," said Rachel's daddy. "This be fine for us now. Your Rachel, she was kind enough to offer it, but my wife and daughter need good shelter, so that be mighty kind of you."

"I have a wife too, when she comes back. Name of Sukey."

"I know that too," said Rachel's daddy.

"So I reckon we're both suited."

"I reckon that be true."

The two men shook hands, and Titan sloped back through the forest in his flimsy shoes, with Rachel slipping and sliding behind him. Why, she reckoned he'd known all the time who the little family was. He must have seen her daddy before, tall and dark and straight-limbed like the man's older daughter. Or maybe he'd spied her little sister, Rachel, who was the dead spit of her. Titan had put two and two together, just like with the colonel's arithmetic. Titan was such a clever man. Rachel wondered now whether she'd needed to tell him anything. Except maybe about the guineas. She wondered too if her confession had changed his course. Maybe he would have thrown her other family out if she hadn't owned up to knowing them. She shivered all the way home.

CHAPTER $V_{''}^{°}$ 9

It was Christmas Eve. Rachel had taught her last class of the year and the children had behaved like a pack of wild dogs. Even little Rachel, who had just joined the others, was giggling and shifting around like she had ants under her backside. Colonel Blucke still hadn't returned and the children thought that gave them a certificate of freedom. Not the slave kind. The school kind. It wasn't that they were excited about Christmas, for in most cases nothing special was promising to come their way. It was that they were mighty pleased to be getting a week off from "the book learnin'," as they now all termed it, courtesy of Hannah. She still managed to say "book learnin'" or "learnin' nonsense," with her nose stuck straight up in the air, as if it were a deathly disease. And since they'd all found out school was a deal harder than they'd expected it to be, they mostly agreed with her.

Still, now they knew their letters all the way to their Y and their Z, which Rachel had taught them this morning. As long as none of the early letters had dropped out of their brains. That was the problem, she sometimes thought. When you pushed one bit of knowledge in, another flew out. You couldn't keep it all in there together unless you maybe locked their heads with a big brass key.

"The Y is like two boughs dividing on a great oak tree. The Z is a big old zag of lightning," she told them, hoping that if they saw those letters as pictures, they would stick. But her voice was a whisper in the din.

"Shut your silly Nigra mouths!" she had yelled suddenly. And they were so shocked they all did, at least for a moment. Then they went back to messing and giggling.

She had almost wept with weariness. "I don't know what to do with these Nigras," she told Ann-Marie, "and with the colonel away I'm not getting any lessons myself." Ann-Marie clucked sympathetically, but said nothing.

Rachel was glad to make her way home with Hannah and Jem. It was a relief to be inside, away from the snow and the naughty children. But even the hut was miserable. The pale tongues of fire licked the smoky lips of the fireplace, but not a shimmer of warmth reached beyond the grate. There was little for dinner, just scant bowls of cornmeal. Nathan Crowley seemed to have forgotten the Sparrows. He hadn't brought any belly-filling food for weeks, nor any other kind neither, no doubt too taken up with Christmas in *his* house to worry about Christmas in theirs. Jem cried and cried, pulling at his gums. Titan sat in a corner, head drooping.

Oh dear. No matter how many people there were in the little hut, it was still dreary as a foggy day. That was because Mamma wasn't there. She'd never come home now. Rachel should have kept that last guinea. It had been a heap of bad luck to give it away. If nothing else, she could have spent it on Christmas. Now they had nothing to look forward to.

Snow was falling through the chimney. The fire sputtered and died. Rachel felt as wretched as she'd ever felt in her whole life, worse even than when she was a slave back in South Carolina.

Suddenly there was a knock at the door. Who could it be, out in this terrible weather? Rachel rushed to open it, hoping against hope to see Mamma. It wasn't Mamma, of course. She was too long gone to turn up on the doorstep like a three-penny piece that had rolled around the table and come back to its owner. But Ann-Marie was standing there with all Rachel's students, Corey and little Rachel among them. They were smiling, didn't seem in the least to mind the snow falling between their necks and collars.

"These children want to tell you something," said Ann-Marie.

Molasses stepped forward. "Please, Miz Rachel, we just want to say we sorry for bein' so bad. Book learnin' is good. Bein' clever Nigras is even better. We can't wait to start school again. Leastways it warm in Massa Blucke's house. And I brought you a special something for bein' so kind to me and mine." Molasses held out a tiny bowl of treacle.

A moment later Nanna Jacklin joined them. "Merry Christmas," she said, holding out a cup of *blackbetty* jam. Rachel took the treacle in one hand, the jam in the other.

"Thank you all very much," she beamed. "It will be a sweet Christmas."

She took the gifts into the house and came straight back. Titan, curious, and Hannah, carrying Jem, came back with her. Other Nigras were beginning to gather, coming to see what all the fuss was about. Among them were Rachel's real true daddy and his wife, who was looking a deal more healthy.

"I brung you this," her daddy said to her, holding out a tiny doll whittled from wood. "I been carrying it about all these years. It wasn't yours, but I fashioned it to be a reminder of you. You be the reason I called my new daughter Rachel. I be pleasantly hoping she grow up like you."

There was a tiny rustle. Glancing sideways, Rachel could see Nathan Crowley hiding behind a tall fir a ways off. She could tell him by his silver-buckled shoes, half buried by snow. They stuck out from the bottom of the tree like roots. He wouldn't reveal himself with all these Nigras around. She'd get to speak to him later though. And she knew he'd have a mound of food for them. How could she have imagined, even for one minute, that he would forget her? Now Rachel was crying. She hadn't realized that so many people cared about her.

"Make way, make way," came a deep growly voice. It was Colonel Blucke, returned at last, just in time for Christmas. The folk of Birchtown separated into two cornrows, waiting for him to pass through. Then Rachel saw. The colonel wasn't riding his great brown horse. He was leading it. Sitting atop the animal, looking more than a mite uncomfortable, was Mamma!

"They beasts sure do make you backside stiff," she complained, sliding off the horse and into the snow with a bump. Rachel and Titan ran to hug her.

After a minute the colonel approached them, speaking so only they could hear. "I traced Miz Sparrow down with the help of the white men's records," he said. "George Gyssop had moved to Halifax. And there's one more thing ..." He seemed to be addressing Rachel.

"Yessuh?" she replied.

*Sitting atop the animal,
looking more than a mite
uncomfortable, was Mamma!*

"I've spoken to the white folk over in Shelburne. They're going to give us money for a school, Rachel Sparrow, a real school. We'll build it soon as the earth warms in spring. I'm to be schoolmaster, but you'll be my assistant. I'll be paying you a shilling a week to get all that learning into those Negro heads."

Rachel gasped. Mamma back. And a whole shilling. And a proper teaching place. She didn't know what to say. So she bobbed a curtsey instead. Colonel Blucke smiled a big friendly smile. It was kind of lopsided, truth to tell, like he wasn't used to creasing his face lately. He led his horse away. The crowd began to disperse.

"Come back later," Rachel whispered to Ann-Marie.

"I'll try. Merry Christmas." Ann-Marie disappeared into the woods, and the Sparrows went indoors. Rachel put her new doll down on the table.

"You never guess what happen," said Mamma. "Colonel Blucke, he talk gruff to that old George

Gyssop, he give him what for and tell him to pay me." Her fingers opened like dark rose petals unfurling. Five golden guineas glinted in her palm. "Bet you never see such money in your whole life, girl," she grinned at Rachel.

"Yes, Mamma. No, Mamma." Rachel smiled a secret smile. "And we got surprises for you too. Just you wait and see." She hugged Mamma again. She thought she'd never get through with hugging her.

At that moment there came a second knock at the door. That would be Nathan, with all their Christmas food. Before letting him in, Rachel looked around. At Mamma, at Titan, at Jem, and at Hannah, who seemed to fit in for good and all. Now that Nathan had turned up, there were just a few more people to come. Rachel's daddy, his wife, and her new little sister. Maybe Ann-Marie too. And Corey and Nanna Jacklin. Then, though times were still mean, for sure there would be frolics tonight: singing and dancing, eating and drinking, jumping up and down with the sheer joy of living. That was the way of it, sure enough. For Rachel. And for her entire elephant tree family.

ACKNOWLEDGEMENTS

MANY THANKS TO MY FAMILY AND FRIENDS;

TO COREY GUY, AND TO CLARA AND EARNESTINE OF THE

JACKLYN FAMILY, ALL DESCENDANTS OF THE

ORIGINAL BLACK LOYALISTS;

TO LAIRD NIVEN, THE ARCHAEOLOGIST OF THE BIRCHTOWN SITE,

AND TO PATRICIA CLARK OF SENECA COLLEGE, WHO WERE

BOTH IMMENSELY HELPFUL;

TO BARBARA BERSON, MY TERRIFIC EDITOR;

TO CINDY KANTOR, WHO BROUGHT THE IDEA FOR

THE SERIES TO PENGUIN;

AND

TO BOOKFRIENDS, WHO ARE ALWAYS AN AMAZING SOURCE OF

SUPPORT AND GOOD HUMOUR.

Dear Reader,

This has been the fourth and final book about Rachel. We hope you've enjoyed meeting and getting to know her as much as we have enjoyed bringing her—and her wonderful story—to you.

Although Rachel's tale is told, there are still eleven more terrific girls to read about, whose exciting adventures take place in Canada's past—girls just like you. So do keep on reading!

And please—don't forget to keep in touch! We love receiving your incredible letters telling us about your favourite stories and which girls you like best. And thank you for telling us about the stories you would like to read! There are so many remarkable stories in Canadian history. It seems that wherever we live, great stories live too, in our towns and cities, on our rivers and mountains. We hope that Our Canadian Girl captures the richness of that past.

Sincerely,
Barbara Berson

1608
Samuel de Champlain establishes the first fortified trading post at Quebec.

1759
The British defeat the French in the Battle of the Plains of Abraham.

1812
The United States declares war against Canada.

1845
The expedition of Sir John Franklin to the Arctic ends when the ship is frozen in the pack ice; the fate of its crew remains a mystery.

1869
Louis Riel leads his Métis followers in the Red River Rebellion.

1871
British Columbia joins Canada.

1755
The British expel the entire French population of Acadia (today's Maritime provinces), sending them into exile.

1776
The 13 Colonies revolt against Britain, and the Loyalists flee to Canada.

1837
Calling for responsible government, the Patriotes, following Louis-Joseph Papineau, rebel in Lower Canada; William Lyon Mackenzie leads the uprising in Upper Canada.

1867
New Brunswick, Nova Scotia and the United Province of Canada come together in Confederation to form the Dominion of Canada.

1870
Manitoba joins Canada. The Northwest Territories become an official territory of Canada.

1762
Elizabeth

Timeline

1885
At Craigellachie, British Columbia, the last spike is driven to complete the building of the Canadian Pacific Railway.

1898
The Yukon Territory becomes an official territory of Canada.

1914
Britain declares war on Germany, and Canada, because of its ties to Britain, is at war too.

1918
As a result of the Wartime Elections Act, the women of Canada are given the right to vote in federal elections.

1945
World War II ends conclusively with the dropping of atomic bombs on Hiroshima and Nagasaki.

1873
Prince Edward Island joins Canada.

1896
Gold is discovered on Bonanza Creek, a tributary of the Klondike River.

1905
Alberta and Saskatchewan join Canada.

1917
In the Halifax harbour, two ships collide, causing an explosion that leaves more than 1,600 dead and 9,000 injured.

1939
Canada declares war on Germany seven days after war is declared by Britain and France.

1949
Newfoundland, under the leadership of Joey Smallwood, joins Canada.

1897
Emily

1885
Marie-Claire

1939
Ellen

Check out the
OUR CANADIAN GIRL website

FUN STUFF

- E-cards
- Contests
- Recipes
- Activities and crafts

FAN AREA

- Fan guest book
- Photo gallery
- Downloadable OUR CANADIAN GIRL
tea party kit

Get to know the girls! What does Angelique dream about? What is most important to Millie? What does Izzie long for?

www.ourcanadiangirl.ca